BITS & PIECES

By
Michelle Chrisner

First Edition

Published by Faith by Grace Publishing

First Faith by Grace Publishing Printing 2015.

All the characters in this book are fictitious. Any resemblance to actual persons, living or dead, is purely coincidental. All work is from the imagination of the author.

ISBN-13: 978-0692530375

ISBN-10: 0692530371

A record of the Library of Congress serial number can be acquired from the publisher.

Manufactured in the United States of America

Cover done by Ashlea Jones

Book layout and design by Ashlea Jones

About the Author

Michelle Chrisner is a horror and suspense drama author, screenwriter and director. Her debut horror novel , *Riker's Point,* was published in 2009, by Wordclay Publishing and her short story, *Propelling Physics,* was included in the anthology *"More Than Meets The Eye"*. She has recently been published in a poem anthology book, *"Soaring High"*. In addition, she had an article published in the MADDvocate magazine and her poetry in *The Victim Service Newsletter.*

Michelle has a passion for screenwriting and has just completed her debut feature length drama/suspense script *"Separate Paths"* and recently directed *"Coffee and Confessions,"* a short film project that aired with Channel Austin. Each of Michelle's projects are full of twists, turns and comedic feel within the characters she creates.

Prelude

Bit's and Pieces is a combination of short stories, poetry and pieces of the author's work. These works of the writings are in different genres. Some stories will become novels, and/or film scripts, while others will be lyrics for songs. This collection of her work is just the beginning. She has more projects that are in the works with drama, horror and suspense.

Table of Content

Overlooked

The big city can bring happiness to the eager, hard worker. The streets are filled with busy people, going here and there with their jumbled schedules that take control of their lives. People too stressed or too focused with their own personal lives to even stop to see what might be standing in front of them or in the shadows of the night.

Brad watches people walk by him without a care in the world. For ten years, he has lived in the trenches on the streets, just trying to survive for his own agenda.

The Blistering wind crystalizes upon Brad's crackling lips. His nose bruises with the stinging wind. He tugs at his blanket that intertwines around his slender body, while his teeth begin to chatter between the beats of his trembling body. With a raspy low voice, he calls for his faithful golden retriever, Spike, "Come here boy. Looks like it's gunna be a long cold night again."

Spike whimpers as he moves closer to Brad's body to keep warm. The dog sniffs at the tattered blanket and buries his nose deeper inside of the material.

The winds pick up, it rattles empty tin cans that are scattered next to a metal dumpster. The can roll along the slick surface of the street and twists around as if it were trying to decide what direction to go in. The cans continue to roll next to a parked car as it rests beneath the tire.

Brad stands up and walks towards the parked car and bends down to pick up the empty can. He looks around his surroundings and holds his head down as he continues back to his spot along the sidewalk. He grasps the can tight until it crushes in on one side and tosses it into the dumpster allowing the tin to clang loudly along the sides of the bulky container.

Footsteps magnify from behind him as a crowd of people exit the movie theatre. Brad slowly moves back to his spot where Spike and his blanket are resting. Brad pulls out a small metal cup from his backpack. His crooked index finger grasps the bent handle as he holds the cup in the air towards the people walking by.

The pedestrians walk by Brad as if he were a permanent fixture of the flaking, brittle brick that forms the wall behind him. A woman walks by him tapping her high heels with every step along the hard, slick surface. She jumps away from Brad as she clings on to her boyfriend's arm, squalling in a high pitched voice, "Ewe! Don't let it touch me!" Her boyfriend pulls her closer, as they look over their shoulders with a sour look on their face. They continue to walk faster away from Brad.

Brad's arm shakes as he holds the cup higher at the crowd; he shouts "A little help here!"

Clang...Clang... as a few coins drop into his cup. Brad looks inside and rocks his cup back and forth like a rattlesnake shakes his rattles before it strikes its prey.

Brad continues his requests, as he demands, "You spend more money on your popcorn than you do for your fellow man!" He begins to rock back and forth while his words slur he chants, "Mary, Mary quite contrary..."

He stands up staggering towards a group of people that have gathered next to a newspaper stand. They laugh and talk among themselves. Brad taps the shoulder of a man who is wearing a dark leather jacket with pleated pants and black shoes that glimmer with the beam of light protruding from the light pole affixed on the sidewalk. Brad demands, "This is my territory! Pay me my dues or get out of here!"

"Excuse me?" The man responds with a stern voice as he raises his hands toward Brad. He continues his conversation, "Uh... Sir...You don't need to come any closer. My colleagues and I are on our way to a late dinner and your foul odor will stain my appetite."

The man's forehead wrinkles and his mouth sours. As he brushes at his jacket, he comments, "How vile! Now I must get my jacket cleaned!" The man gazes back at Brad focusing on his worn out boots, that are exposing his toes and then gazes at his hair, that is matted to his head with patches of his short locks sticking straight up.

The man's voice softens as he confronts Brad. "Now look here mister. I'll give you something, but you must go away. I won't give you cash, hell from the smell of you, you'd probably spend it on alcohol." He reaches inside his jacket and swiftly pulls out a business card, he scribbles on the back of it. He flicks the card towards Brad, he makes sure he doesn't have physical contact with his body. The man explains, "If you need to get some kind of nourishment for tonight and maybe get out of this blistering cold weather, make your way down second street then go right on University Avenue. There you will find Marilio's on the corner. Show the card to the personnel inside. Tell them Frankie sent you; they will set you up for tonight." Frankie winks at Brad and walks away with his friends across the street. He turns around as he yells, "But for God's sake man! Put yourself through a car wash before you start allowing my name to come out your mouth."

Brad gazes at the business card, flipping it over and over between his dirty fingers. He cups his hand around his mouth and yells out, "For God's sake? I wouldn't be in this mess if it weren't for God forgetting about me!" He rubs hard at the side of his face and strokes at his scraggly beard. He starts to mumble, "I don't want a hand out from a silver spoon fed snob!"

His callous hand crinkles the card into a ball as he places it into the pocket of his tattered jacket. His whiskey bottle hidden inside of his jacket invites his taste buds as he pulls the half empty bottle out from the pocket. His fingers tremble while he tries to unscrew the cap and he begins to ramble about Frankie's assumption of his drinking. He mumbles "You don't know nothing... with your fancy, smanchie clothes...huh." He takes a quick swig of his whiskey while he starts to chant, "Mary...Mary...you're quite contrary." He takes another swig from the bottle and coughs, wiping his mouth with the sleeve of his jacket.

Brad staggers back to his spot along the brick wall. He buries himself under the blanket as he holds on to Spike. He closes his eyes as he huffs, "How do you expect a man to survive these cold nights without my warming drink?"

****

The early morning arises while the sun cascades out from the clouds. It beams through the small empty space between the buildings across the street. Footsteps magnify loudly in Brad's ears while he slowly emerges out from his blanket. He stretches out his arms and yawns, scratching at his beard as he tries to get the hair to lay in one direction.

Spike jumps onto his lap and excitedly licks his face. Brad chuckles, "Ha, ha, ha…okay boy! Let's go get you something to eat. The chow truck won't stay in one place for long." He rolls up his blanket, neat and tidy. He reaches in his backpack and he pulls out a rusted chain, hooking it onto Spike's collar. They both walk down the street towards the backed up traffic of cars and busses waiting their turn for the green light.

Eager shop keepers, in front of their doorways, along the busy street can be seen pouring sand and salt on the remnants of the ice build up from the over night hours. Several security gates grind along the metal tracks while the panels are being unlocked and retracted exposing the business' storefront windows.

A rush of business suits and clunky briefcases come in waves down the sidewalks making it impossible to infiltrate the front lines walking in the opposite direction. Whistles echo down the street as some pedestrians hail taxicabs.

Brad fumbles for his cup while extending his arm out towards the pedestrians walking by. He rattles his cup, that has a few coins inside, hoping to catch their attention. A man walks by jiggling some coins in his pant's pocket. He reaches over towards Brad's cup, but quickly retreats his gestures. He snaps his fingers at Brad as if he were a dog. The man demands, "Go get a job like everyone else!"

A woman with blonde hair and earrings that dangle from her thick earlobes walks by Brad. Her shiny bracelets cover both of her wrists and forearms. They clatter together as she jumps away from him. She looks him up and down and says, "This is disgusting! The trash should have already been taken away last night. I feel sorry for your dog! I would adopt him, but I'm afraid you might have given him rabies!"

Brad spits on the ground in her direction, batting the air with his hands as he huffs, "Stop telling your friends that you have a real job and go work your corner, girl!"

Brad stomps away from the impossible crowd and walks around the corner. A roar from an engine rumbles the ground. Brad becomes frantic as he runs towards the constant throttling. "Oh no! We aren't going to make it!" he says, running towards the truck with the draw doors being closed and locked. The light crowd dissipates from around the rumbling truck. Brad yells, "Wait! Please, don't leave yet!"

He runs towards the cab of the truck. The driver's side door creaks open as the driver's head peers out he asks, "What's your problem?"

Brad replies, "You scoundrel! Don't leave! My dog needs to eat!"

The driver looks back inside of the cab and tosses a half eaten burger at Spike. With a chuckling voice he says, "Sorry, we have a schedule to keep. Next time you panhandle, ask someone for a watch, that way you'll be on time for our delivery." The driver slams the cab door and drives off, slinging small pebbles out from his tires.

Brad grabs his heart and stands still as if he were paralyzed. He takes in a deep breath and mumbles, "Those no good son-of – bitches! This country is going to hell in a hand basket!"

He bends down and pats the top of Spike's head. He whispers, "Come on boy. Let's go make our rounds. Let's get cleaned up, so that maybe a shop keeper will let you have some water."

He grabs ahold of his whiskey bottle and begins his morning ritual. Spike whimpers as the whiskey dribbles out of the corner of Brad's lips and spills on his jacket.

The crumbled up business card that Frankie had given to him had stuck to the bottom of Brad's whiskey bottle and fell in front of Spike. Brad moans and groans while he bends down to pick it up off of the ground. He chuckles, "Hey boy, trash just seems to follow us..don't it boy?" He pats Spike's head and tries to straighten the card. He pauses for a moment and closes his eyes while he gasps, "Well, we need to get you some food. These gosh, darn frozen nights are gunna kill us both for sure if we don't get a full belly soon." He pulls at Spike's leash and walks down the sidewalk.

They walk eight blocks down and turn right on University Avenue. He pulls on the cold handle of the door and enters the building.

A worker trots fast towards the front door waving his hands at Brad and commands, "Whoa...whoa! You can't come in here!"

Brad starts to explain, "I have a..."

"No need to say anything else, you need to leave! We open in fifteen minutes and we don't need to scare away our customers," the worker explained.

Brad scratches his beard and begins to chant, "Mary...Oh Mary...Why are you so contrary?" He holds out his hand and exposes the crinkled business card and demands, "Take it! I got it from Frankie."

The worker surprisingly asks, "From Frankie? Are you sure?"

In a frustrating voice Brad answers, "Yes, I didn't stutter. Frankie."

"Well, come in and head to the back. Be quick about it, you're leaving a heavy stink in here," comments the worker.

Brad and Spike make their way to the back of the building. Brad pulls out a rickety old wooden chair and sits down tugging at his shirt. His rough fingers graze across the wood's grain, on top of the table, as he whispers, "Nice...red wood...what a great choice."

A cook peers out from the door and yells back into the kitchen, "Yo..we got another..looks like two this time."

Brad stares across the room, as his eyes begin to shut, he listens to the clanging inside of the kitchen as if it were a soft lullaby soothing a baby to sleep.

"Excuse me?" whispers Roxie. She taps Brad on his shoulder, with her dainty fingers, as she whispers again, "Sir, here is your food. Let me know if you need anything else. Oh, and I gave your dog some scraps from the kitchen." Roxie smiles as she ties her half apron around her waist and picks up a stack of serving trays from the rack.

Brad holds his hand in the air, "Thank you for your kindness, it's been along time since I have been served inside of a building. And Spike thanks you." He leans down close to the steaming, hot food on his plate. He takes in a deep breath, through his nose, and begins to eat his food slowly, enjoying every bite.

Roxie smiles, "I noticed you admiring the table, did you work with wood in the past?"

Brad leans back in his chair and dabs the napkin on his mouth. His eyebrows begin to rise and his eyes widen. He clears his throat, "Well...Yes..I used to build top of the line office furniture. You know, the kind that business owners would salivate over just to earn their clout with their business."

Roxie's forehead wrinkles, "How come you are on the streets and not making furniture?"

Brad chuckles roughly, "Sweetie..life becomes a wedge with people's hopes and dreams. Some times doing the right thing can make a person look lazy and incompetent with their talents. And eventually they become angry and bitter at this unjust world."

Roxie looks around the room and walks closer to Brad. Her voice becomes quiet and she asks, "Can I ask ...why do you choose to live this way, when you can work?"

Brad sops up the last bit of gravy with his biscuit as he stands up from his chair. He winks at Roxie and heads for the back door, grumbling as he turns around he says, "Well ma'am, thank you for your conversation with me, but I have over stayed my welcome." He whistles at Spike and they walk outside of the building.

■■■

Brad walks outside while car horns honk, sounding from a few blocks away. Brad holds onto his ears, swinging his head around to face away from the sounds. The light pierces his eyes as if they were a route straight into the sun. Spike dashes out into the alley and barks as he runs around the corner.

Brad excitedly yells, "Spike! Come here! Spike!" He stumbles into the exterior wall as his hands guide his footing with every touch of the crumbling brick. "Spike! Where are you boy?" he commands.

Brad follows the echoing barks that bounce through the narrow alleys. He moves swiftly to catch up to the sound. The cars whisk by as Brad frantically gazes left, then right. He squints his eyes as he tries to block the bright sunray that blinds his vision.

"There you are boy! What has gotten into you?" Spike whimpers as his tail retreats between his legs.

A bright glow peers through the congested clouds as it beams on the tip of the cobblestone cross that rests on the top of the church's highest peek on the roof.

Brad's body becomes paralyzed as his eyes fixate on the vibrant colors that are protruding out from the cross. His body becomes magnified towards the church's door as he wants to turn and run, but his feet are embedded onto the weather worn doorway. His hands shake while he gently caresses the stain glass that reflects on his fingers. His arms push on the doors as his mind wanders into a foggy sensation. The door creaks open while the screeching sound magnifies slowly into his ear, and his heart pounds inside of his chest. His vision remains blocked as he gazes left, then right with his breath becoming short. Brad's voice cracks becomes a high pitch as he nervously speaks, "Hello? Is anyone one here?"

His voice bounces off the marbled glazed walls, while a few small candles flicker in the front row of pews that rest uniformed in the chapel. A soft whimper emerges from the dimmed area of the pews.

"Hello? Someone in here?" Brad slowly asks. The whimpers become silent as he nears the fourth pew from the front of the room. "Hello?" He asks while his fingers squeak along the polished mahogany wood. His eyes widen as he tries to get a closer look to match the whimpering sound.

A little girl peeks out from the seat of the pew as she sniffs her nose and wipes at her face with the sleeve of her shirt. Her shoulder length, blonde hair glimmers with the beams of light protruding through the angelic stain glass window behind her.

Brad looks behind him and back at the girl. He scratches his hair and rubs at his face, he whispers, "Why are you crying? Are your parents here?"

She looks up at Brad with her blue eyes and shakes her head no as she sniffs her nose. She grasps her small brown teddy bear tightly into her arms.

"Well... What do you have there? Is that your friend? What's his name?"

The little girl mumbles, "It's a girl."

"You must excuse me, I'm a little hard of hearing. This old body ain't what it use to be. What did you say?"

The little girl stands on her tip toes and cradles her mouth with her hands as she shouts, "I said, it's a girl, Mandy!"

"Aw…a girl, yes, now I see the bow. Well, do you think Mandy will tell this old coot why this pretty little blue eyed girl is crying?"

She places the teddy bear in front of her face and then next to her ear. She gazes at the ground as she takes in a deep breath. She softly responds, "Mandy said she may have gotten lost from her family. She was at the park and saw a puppy and followed it down the street."

"I see…Well…Maybe Mandy will let me find someone to help her back to her bear family. Do you think she will let me help her?"

The little girl stares at the teddy bear and hugs it tight. She smiles and answers, "We aren't supposed to be with strangers."

Brad looks up at the ceiling, rubs the back of his neck and chuckles under his breath. "I too don't enjoy being around strangers, they aren't very nice at times are they?" He brushes off his clothes and holds out his dirty hand towards the little girl. "My name is Brad and I really could use a friend for my dog, Spike. Have you seen my dog? He too could be lost around here, just like Mandy. What's your name?"

She bats her eyes and places the bear's fluffy paw on Brad's hand. With a high pitch voice as she mimics a cartoon voice, "My name is Mandy and this is my buddy Verna."

"See… Now, we aren't stranger's anymore. Let's look around this church to see if anyone else can be our friend, okay?"

Verna quickly nods her head yes and keeps her teddy bear to the side of her while Brad continues to hold on to it's paw. They walk towards the front of the chapel and through the opened door behind the pulpit. The hallway becomes bright with florescent lights and the floor is cushioned with blue/gray carpet.

"Hello?" Brad yells out. "Anyone here?"

"Can I help you?" Brad hears, as a man peers from an office room.

Brad begins to quickly chatter, "I'll get out of here as soon as I get this girl some help. I won't touch anything in here, nor will I steal it."

The man smiles "Sir, please, slow down. I'm brother Gary, the pastor for this church. What can I help you with?"

Brad scratches his cheek and explains, "Verna, this little girl right here, told me that her teddy bear has gotten lost from the park and she has allowed me to find someone to help her find their family."

"I understand sir. And I thank you for your concern for this child's well being." Gary responded.

Brother Gary reaches inside of his pocket and pulls out a cell phone and dials quickly. He nods and winks at Brad. Gary calmly speaks into the phone. "Yes. This is

Brother Gary at the 2nd street Church. I have a lost, little girl needing to find her family. She has Shoulder length, blonde hair. She is wearing a pink and white t-shirt and blue jeans. The shoes? It looks like they are a dark blue with pink polka dots. Uh huh...Okay...That's wonderful. Yes, we will be at this location. Thank you and God bless you."

Brother Gary pats Brad on his shoulder and softly speaks to Verna. "Greats news! Your mother is on her way to pick you up. It seems she has been looking for you all over the park and found an officer on a bicycle who rode on all of the bike paths to help her find you. Would you like to play in this room until she gets here? You can draw on the chalk board if you like."

Verna nods her head and claps her hands with excitement. "I like to draw," she exclaimed.

Brother Gary picks up the box of chalk and allows the chalk sticks to clang together in his hands. "Well, look at this...I bet you will like this pink colored chalk to draw with."

Verna stands on her tiptoes to look at the chalk, she gently grasps the pink one. She races over to the chalkboard and begins to draw clouds and trees.

Brother Gary turns towards Brad and gazes at his clothing. "I don't mean to offend you, but we have some clothing that people have donated, across the hall, if you would like to go check it out and keep anything that fits you."

Brad closes his eyes and huffs, "I don't want to bother you. I know I'm an eye sore in your building, so I will be on my way."

Brother Gary waves his hands out in front of him, "No..please, you don't have to leave." He says. "This is the house of the Lord, not my building. Anyone is welcome in this house. Actually, I'm impressed with your outreach for this young girl that needed help. I believe you were guided here for a reason. I'm also in need of a helper around the church, if you would like to help. You know, just wipe down the woodwork and tidy up the offices? "

Brad takes a step backwards and scratches his head.

Brother Gary softly chuckles, "It doesn't pay much, but you can have room and board here. I know you will do a great job. What do you say?"

"I have only one condition. I have my friend with me, Spike... he's a dog. I need him with me." Brad explained.

"I wouldn't think of splitting up a family. Absolutely, Spike can help you here too. Maybe a little later we can sit and chat for awhile."

Brad cracks a half smile across his face as he roughly laughs, "Brother, I think maybe our chat needs to be extended by clearing your calendar for a month, and that's just me getting started."

Brother Gary firmly shakes Brad's hand, "Well, you just let me know when you are ready. I will clear my calendar for a year if needed."

Brad enters a restroom to change into a blue button down, long sleeve shirt and black slacks. He places his foot into shiny black loafers as he takes in a deep breath, "Aw, that feels so good, cushiony insoles." He places his hands under the warm stream of water that is filtrating from the faucet and slicks his hair back to make the strands of hair rest flat on his head. He gazes at the mirror as it reflects Brad's sparkling eyes and a glowing smile across his face.

Brad walks out of the church and is greeted by Spike jumping on his hind legs as Brad pats his fur in a playful manner. "Come on boy! Looks like our luck is changing. Let's head down the road a bit. I've got our usual stop to make."

Brad clips the rusted chain to Spike's collar and walks down the road. They make their way through the crowded sidewalks. Brad seemed to be fast and light on his feet. He double checks his looks when some of the people say hello to him and kindly bump up next to him as they make their way through the crowds.

Brad and Spike find an elevator that allows them access in the lobby of a hospital building. The elevator heads up to the fifth floor as it rumbles, tickling Brad's feet.

The doors beep and squeak open. The bright floor tiles shine in his eyes as he struggles to view the faded black numbers on the individual doors. 521 appears in his vision and he grazes his fingers across the numbers. He slowly opens the door.

The beeps from the machines echo around the room. The breathing machine pumps and swishes loudly, clicking with every breath as it rises for the next push of air. Tears fill Brad's eyes as he softly strokes his wife's silvery brown hair while she lies in the bed with no kind of movement. "Mary... Oh Mary... You still lay here so still. Why are you so contrary?" He gently cradles her pale dainty hand resting ay the side of her body. His lips savor every second as he places her hand to his kiss. "I miss you so much sweetheart. I've done all I can. I've sold our house, everything that we have owned, even sold the clothes on my back to pay for you to stay here, hoping that one day you will open your eyes and we can live our lives together again. This has been a long 10 years with the bitter cold nights and the abomination I have endured from others it has left me a bitter old man, until today. I still have nothing left to offer you but my love...I realized that I have surrendered all of my material things to keep you safe, but I went about it all wrong! It's not the money or where I sleep or the food I eat, nor the fancy clothes I may wear...It's about God and what he wants. I needed to realize that I can't do this on my own and I do need help, even if my mind says otherwise. God still has you here, alive in this bed, waiting for my stubbornness to end. Mary, I need you, I love you! Oh God! Please hear this old coot. I'm not a perfect man, but please complete me; I surrender to you with what ever you call on me to do. Please bring my Mary back to me. I'm not strong enough to take this pain in my soul no longer! I need her love to embrace me again. God, if you wish to take her do it now, but end my life as well. I can't live without her anymore. Please forgive my ignorance and stubbornness, Lord."

Brad weeps continuously as he embraces Mary grasping her body tight, and closes his eyes in exhaustion for a few minutes that seem to stretch into hours. The beeping from the machine marches at a faster pace.

Brad feels a slight pressure run across his hairline and down his face. He slowly opens his eyes and blinks them quickly as he tries to sharpen his vision. A pale dainty hand peers from a warm, bright light that cascades over Mary. She caresses his head. "Mary! What? Oh my...I can't believe it! You're here! And awake! Oh sweetheart, I love you so much!" Tears flow down his face as he holds onto Mary while her arms grasp his trembling body. "Everything is going to be okay now, Mary. We are in God's hands...Yes, we are."

Why does this curse keep following us?

One down, two down, three and four.
Nobody knows how many more.
The two were first to go that stunned us all and stopped illegal actions
for a short haul.

But once forgotten, all continued.
Two young brothers thought they were invincible.

Why does this continue? Do people really care?
Why must they be so unaware?

This won't be the last one to fall to a disease that will surely kill us all.
Four young cousins killed by the devil's drink.
I wonder who will be the next to sink.
If we don't stand up and fight, who will be left to tell their children good night?

Someday

Some days I feel like crying.
Other days I may be whining.
I don't know how to feel.
Is this really real?

One day, will it be you standing with me.
Secrets of the heart, that could break apart,
if you were to know when my feelings will show.

One day, someday, it will be,
you lying next to me.
One day, some day it will be.

Afraid of you saying no.
Time has gone by, with you trapped inside.
The wind blowing on my face, so numb I can't embrace.
Wishing you were near, to stop all my tears.

You are the light flickering in my life.
I know it will survive.

One day, some day.
It will be the right time, right place,
to open my arms, my heart, my space.
One day, some day.
The right time, the right place.

Unspeakable Thoughts

The phone rang early in the morning as if it were the church bells ringing that called for the congregation to appear. Shawn jumped up as if he were a dolphin in a fish show.

He answered his phone, "Hello, hey, yeah it's me. Are you ready? Okay, I'll be there."

Shawn's wife Adriana emerged from her sleep slowly because of her long tiring hours at work and taking care of their four -year old daughter.

"Who was that?" she asked.

"Oh, just a few people from work wanting to play a few rounds of paintball at the course," Shawn replied.

"I thought we had plans for our anniversary today? Why do you always go off with your co-workers by yourself? You know, I work with them too!" Adriana exclaimed.

She stood up in front of him and glared into his eyes. She said, "Oh I see, she is going to be there! I can't believe you are still cheating on me! I do everything for you, I work six days a week, I clean the house, cook your meals, I watch our daughter and you just go off when ever you feel like it and go see all of your little girlfriends!" She said angrily.

"No sweetie, I've changed. I only cheated on you because you always took me back. Come with me to the paintball course and play with us if you don't trust me," Shawn exclaimed.

"Fine, I think I will enjoy popping a few rounds," She replied as she brushed her hair with frustration and hit her head with every stroke.

Shawn and Adriana drove to the paintball course. Her co-workers greeted Adriana instantly as they exited the car.

"Hey girl, I'm glad you showed up to play today. I want to be on your team," Cassie said.

Mandy yelled, "Yes! I want to be on your team too. You're a perfect shot Adriana."

Adriana excitedly hugged them and replied, "Thanks you all, let's go get our gear, suit up and be ready to kick some booty."

At the gear booth it seemed to have rows of unending paintball pistols and rifles just ready for the taking.

There were colorful clear buckets of blue, green, yellow, purple and red paintballs that filled the counter. Adriana's group stared at the buckets as if children they were in a candy store not being able to choose which piece of the sweet enjoyment they wanted to eat.

"Hey Adriana," Mandy said as she tapped her on the shoulder. "What is that thing doing here?" she asked.

Adriana turned around and watched Shawn approach Teri. Adriana stroked the long barrel rifle with the automatic trigger. She glanced through the scope and responded politely, "I'll take this one."

She glanced one more time through the scope and focused on Shawn and Teri as they giggled and flirted. They blushed with every eye glance that they made to each other.

Adriana slung her rifle around her shoulder and confidently walked up to her husband. She said, "Say honey, would you like to be on the winning team with me? Or take your chances with this group?" as she showed up Teri.

Shawn walked Adriana to the side away from Teri and asked, "Why did you do that? She's not bothering you!"

Adriana stepped forward to be nose-to-nose with her husband and responded, "I don't like her! I don't like you flirting with her. She is nothing but trash. She sleeps with anything that moves! Why don't you spend some time with me instead of showing off for her?"

"Baby you are imaging things. I love you. Look, I wanted to give my one and only something today. He pulled out a red rose from the inside of his jacket. "To my beautiful wife, a rose just for you." He said.

Adriana looked a little embarrassed and felt foolish. Maybe she had read more into things than what had been really going on. "I'm sorry honey, I should trust you. I love you too," she said as she kissed him on his lips.

"Okay, go with your team and have fun," Shawn replied as he walked back to his group.

Mandy slapped Adriana on her lower back and said, "Don't worry about that slut, we will let you go after her on the course."

"Ha, ha. Yeah, that sounds like a great match up," Adriana said as she rolled her eyes.

Both groups of players put on their color armbands and protective gear. The sound of the paintball guns that were being loaded made constant noises as if popcorn was popping in a movie theatre.
The whistle blew as the instructor of the course explained the rules and time limits for the game.

"Okay. Get to your home base and wait for the horn to blow, then it's game on," explained the instructor.

Both groups made it to their home base and the horn sounded.

"Cassie come with me, Mandy you fall behind us and cover the rear," Adriana directed.

They jogged through the thick part of the woods as the rest of their group tackled the open range. The whirling of the bullets could be heard as if busy bees flew by headed straight for their flowers. Cassie moved forward as she lifted up the branches so that Adriana could grab on to it without causing abrupt movements from the brush. Adriana looks back for Mandy to check for her location.

"PSS," Cassie whispered. "I think I see your husband. He just went behind that fallen shack. I'll let you take that shot and I will cover you," she said.

"Okay," Adriana said as she jogged along the edge of the woods to get a cleaner shot.

She squatted down and raised her rifle with a steady arm and aimed it center mass on her husband. Her finger grazed the trigger lightly as if a soft feather blew in the wind. Just as she was ready to fire and eliminate her opponent, Teri appeared from around the other side of the fallen shack.

Teri ran to Shawn and hugged him tight and rubbed her hands down his back.
Shawn stepped away from her.

"Good boy," Adriana comments.

Shawn reached into the inside of his jacket and pulled out another red rose. He smelled the tip of the rose and placed it on the side of Teri's cheek. They giggled as Shawn fell backwards and grabbed Teri to allow her to fall on top of him. Teri removed his safety goggles and kissed him on the lips.

Adriana couldn't believe what she had seen. She said to her self, "Why did I ever take him back? That son of a bitch! And he is messing with that disease-infected whore! Well, it's going to end now!" as she placed her rifle on the ground she reached into her combat boot and pulled out a bowie knife. She held the handle in her hand with the blade of the knife resting upward along her forearm. She crept up to where Shawn and Teri were still engaged with their kissing. Adriana swiftly straddled Teri's back as she pulled her head backwards and ran the slick blade from the knife across her neck. She tossed Teri's limp body to the side.

"No! Baby! It's not what you think! Come on, I love you. Please think about this," Shawn screamed as he pleaded for his life.

Adriana knelt down and sat upon him. She moved in closer to almost lie upon him. She stroked his sweat filled hair and whispered, "No more lies, honey, it has always been what I thought. You took my heart out and stomped all over it, now I will have yours," as she slammed the blood covered knife into his heart.

Adriana stood up over Shawn and with a blank stare she looked at her blood stained hands. The noises from all around her became muffled and she saw everything as if in slow motion.

"Adriana, Adriana!" Cassie said as she tapped her shoulder to get her to snap out of it.

Adriana shook her head to rattle her mind back to normal. "What did you say?" she asked.

"I said are you going to take your shot? Go get them and hit them hard!" demanded Cassie.

Adriana looked puzzled and glanced at her hands that were clean and still held her rifle with the crosshairs on the target of Shawn and Teri.
Adriana gripped tightly on to her rifle and stomped towards Shawn and Teri as if she had a ton of bricks in her boots.

"Get off of him you slut!" yelled Adriana.

She pointed her rifle at Teri and pulled the trigger without hesitation and sprayed the paintball ammunition all over Teri's face. Adriana looked down at her husband in disgust.

"Get up you coward!" Adriana demanded.

"No sweetie, you are reading into this all wrong," Shawn said as he waved his hands.

"I sure did read into our marriage wrong! It's over for good," Adriana said as she moved in closer. She lowered her rifle towards the ground.

"See baby, I knew you would come to your senses," he said.

With a half- cocked smile, Adriana clicked the trigger back on her rifle and let loose her ammunition. She raised her arm and guided the rifle towards her husband at point blank range and pounded the paintballs between his legs.

He tried to cover himself with his hands against the hard pounding paintballs that were a non- stop force between his legs. He screamed in pain as if a little girl would after seeing a spider crawl on her arm.

Adriana tossed her rifle on the ground next to her husband whom had laid down in the fetal position.

"Good luck having anymore kids!" Adriana said as she tossed her wedding ring into the puddle of red paint that soaked her husband's pants while her eyes gleamed with joy.

The Dream

Soldiers trending these muddy streams and bomb at their
reach.
The wars are here and overseas, wondering when this
madness will cease.
With our flags raised high, soon there will be peace.

But here and abroad there is war all around.
Fighting the storms and faith that has come down.

The truth be known, there is one no other.
It's our brave American soldiers.
The fight in their eyes will never die.
There is no other, the heart of this machine, it's the
American dream.

She's mopping the floor, trying to get it clean.
Sweeping away what is left from the hurricane.
It took three houses and her neighbors down the road.
With the fight in her eyes, a soldier she stands with this
beaten up land.

There is no other, a hard working mother.
The heart of this machine gives her what she needs.
It's the American dream.

As the night gets darker, the street becomes mean.
With deadly gangs and blood at our feet.
Many make a stand from senseless act that need to be
banned.
Bring back the hope that we will stay strong.
It's in all of us, living on this land.

The American dream, there is no other.

It's a fighting machine.
It's hard working mothers.
It's people who choose to do the right thing.
We are the American dream.

How will I know?

Sitting here in the dark, wonder where you are.
I must be out of my mind, thinking that you can be mine.

When I look in your eyes, I'm filled with butterflies.
Don't know what to say, to keep myself at bay.

Why does this never happen to me?
To have someone to hold, to call you my very own.

I really do have something to prove, that love is in heart,
but it's being torn apart.

When will it be? How will I know?
How can I show?
That love is really in me.
There is a light that slowly shows.
Do I grab and take ahold or step back into the cold?
How will I see that love is for me?

You captured my heart, but have a life of your own.
Do I tell you today or keep you far away?

When will it be? How will I know?
How can I show that love is really in me?

SPELL BOUNDED

The setting of the sun cascades in Kenny's room. His eyes bury deep within his arms that rests on his soft pillow.

"Kenny?" whispers Veronica. She tip toes on the floor as the wood cracks beneath her soft feet. She whispers again, "Are you a sleep? I keep thinking about Murphy, I can't believe we won't be able to play Frisbee with him anymore."

Kenny wipes the tears from his face as he begins to get frustrated; "Is that all you're going to remember of him, is what he played? What about the time he pulled us out of the icy banks when we fell in, or how he slept on the edge of my bed since I was 2?"

Veronica's eyes fill with tears as she cries, "I miss him too! You don't have to be so mean!"

Kenny sits up on his bed as he gazes at Veronica with her face buried beneath her dainty hands as she sobs uncontrollably. He pats the empty spot next to him on the bed and whispers, "I miss him too, and I just wish he was still here."

Footsteps echo quickly as it pounds on the floor. "Clomp..clomp..clomp," sounds near Kenny's bedroom door. Connie peers from around the corner fumbling through several books in her hands. "Okay kiddos, what story do you want me to read to you tonight?" she asked.

Veronica jumps up with excitement as she bounces on her legs on the springy mattress, she smiles. Kenny points towards the small night stand next to his bed as he requests, "I found this book today near the old saw mill, laying by the creek, can you read this one to us mom...please?"

Veronica excitedly jumps up, and down higher on the bed as she begs, "Oh please mommy, read it...read it...Please?"

A smile penetrates Connie's stern face as she gently caresses Veronica's long, soft hair, her voice trembles; "Seeing you kids perk up even if it is for just a moment, warms my heart. You will always be my sweet little, bundles of joy." She says, picking up the book from the nightstand and opens the hard, dusty cover as the spine crinkles loudly. "Now, let's see what this story has in store for us."

Her guided breath blows across her warm lips as the dust spirals off the top of the delicate pages. She flattens the pages with the tips of her fingers to keep it open. She gazes at the children's eyes and asks in excitement, "Okay...Are you ready? Are you sure you want me to read this?"

Kenny and Veronica quickly settle down under the blanket just as a rabbit snuggles in the brush with their young at night. Veronica quickly claps her hands as her voice fills with anticipation, "Yes! Mommy..read it...I can't wait!"

Connie's voice softens as she begins to read the faded print on the pages of the book: "The riverbanks flow with small waves as sparkling green, and blue rocks glow, that embed in the mud. The trees that align the brush line twist, and turn allowing the long tailed fairies to swing from tree to tree as if they were chimpanzees in a zoo. In the mist of the woods, rests unicorns that have a unique horn that releases a glittery liquid when the herd is at play. King Alvery, and Queen Martice rule the land as they keep very strict enforcement of a law that protects the unicorns. No one is allowed to own, hunt or capture the unicorns; any one caught breaking this law is vanquished into the serpent's swaps where there is no escape from certain death.

Deep in the caverns just passed the serpent swamp lives an evil witch, Zulo. Her skin burns in the daylight if it pierces her scales that run up along her arms and lower back. Her tongue slivers into two as if a snake is feeling it's way along ground. Zulo has kidnapped King Alvery, and Queen Martice in hopes of forcing them to change the law to hunt the unicorns. If they do not agree with her commands, Zulo has created a potion to turn the King, and Queen into crystals, where she will keep them in a jar for later use for her spells to control the unicorn's abundance of the glittery liquid to have longer lasting affects of her spells."

Connie concentrates on the content in the book as she continues to read a sample of Zulo's spell. Her pronunciation is choppy as she says;

"Brandon...bow...chattering
winds, the mind wanders...with every spin...alla
crum..tata blum..stranded crum..now
it's done."

Connie's eyebrows rise as her forehead wrinkles in confusion; "What does this mean?"

Kenny rubs his small finger along the protruded print on the paper, and mumbles; "The words are bumpy too, let's read it again."

Connie, Veronica, and Kenny slowly repeat the spell again at the same time as if their mouths were full of molasses. Suddenly, a tiny, purple, and pink whirlwind appears from the spine of the book. It grows larger with every second, captivating Kenny, and Veronica's attention.

Connie drops the book on the floor and steps back as she yells, "Get away from it, now!"

The whirlwind's top expands as if the potter collapses his wet, clay masterpiece as he spins his creation from the potting wheel. Pictures that hang on the wall, fly through the air, and crashes to the ground as the glass shatters into tiny pieces. Veronica jumps towards her mother and she hangs on to her torso tightly. The whirlwind expands, cascading over Connie, and her children as the strong force from inside of the tunnel collapses into the book.

Connie opens her eyes, and feels the cold, wet mud on her face with her dainty fingers. She frantically looks around for Kenny, and Veronica. She calls out, "Kenny! Verna! Where are you? Hello?"

An echo sounds from the brush, just past the twisty trees. Connie rushes to the edge of the trees as she swats the air in front of her face. Her voice trembles, "Darn flies...Kenny, baby where are you? Verna sweetheart please answer me."

A high pitch, squeaky voice answers; "There over there."

"Who said that?" she responds as she swats the air again.

"Eeeek," sounds flying across her ear.

"Hey, watch those logs of an arm, your hurting my brother," another squeaky voice hollers out.

Connie holds her arms still as if she were frozen in time. Her hands shake as she whispers; "What is going on?"

Her eyes widen, focusing on the tiny, flying fairies. They each had different colors on their body. One has blue spots mixed in with yellow, and short orange hair that has bangs pointing down over its eyes. Another fairy has red spots with a purple body, and short yellow hair. Both fairies have two sets of wings, fluttering in two different directions to keep them in a hovering state.

"I must have hit my head, I'm seeing things," she said, scratching the side of her head.

"Mommy. Mommy, look what I found," as Veronica holds up a leaf as big as her hand. She blows the end of the stem of the leaf. The leaf lights up in a yellow-green glow as tiny bubbles bloom out from its creases.

The fairies fly on top of the leaf, scrambling all over each other to eat the bubbles that were forming. The purple fairy licks his hands as a cat licks the fur on his paws, he squeaks: "Awww. thank you, much appreciated, it takes us days to get our food from these leaves; you made it look so easy...We have been on a long, and tiring journey. The evil witch, Zulo, has taken our King, and Queen. But she lives near the serpent swamps, and we are forbidden to go in there. Our flight doesn't work in that realm, and that allows us to be easy bait for the golden serpent. You look like a good size warrior... Can you help us find our King, and Queen before Zulo launches her powers that will ultimately destroy our land?"

Kenny stands next to his mother, and nudges her side, "Come on mom, let's help. Besides, maybe these fairies can help us find a way back home."

Connie puts her hands on her hips, and gasps, "We aren't trained to fight a witch, nor battle a serpent. I mean really, I am talking to a purple fairy, and Verna is blowing bubbles from a leaf, this is just not possible."

Veronica's eyes fill with tears as she grabs ahold of her mother's hand; "Please momma, I want to go back home, can we try?"

Connie takes in a deep breath and grasps Veronica's cheeks as she strokes her chin with her fingers she says, "Well, okay. Let's do this, but quickly, I'm not sure what kind of dangers are around us."

Connie, Kenny, and Veronica follow behind the fairies as they lead the way towards the serpent swamp. The thick, mucky, water sloshes beneath their feet. Kenny loses his balance as he steps towards the patches of brush along the edge of the water as molding vines wrap around his legs. He leaps out of the tangling vines, brushing away with his hands and feet the debris that is floating on top of the water.

Connie picks up Veronica, and carries her on her shoulder as she follows Kenny through the muddy water. The fairies fly near Connie as they land on Veronica's shoulders. The fairies crawl quickly under Veronica's hair so that they are hidden from any dangers.

Thick fog starts to form over the water, as it becomes difficult to see what lies ahead. Kenny stops walking as he whispers; "I can't see anything...shh. What's that noise?"

Connie looks around her as she grabs onto Veronica tighter; "We need to keep moving...hey little men. Where do we go?"

The orange haired fairy shakes his head pulling at his wings. He squeaks; "We don't know where to go, we are forbidden to enter the serpent swamp.... Good idea, keep moving, so this fog doesn't consume us."

Kenny asks, "Do you hear that mom? The sound, it's getting closer."

Connie responds, "No, I don't hear anything." Veronica whispers, "Mommy, I hear something too. It's right in front of us!"

"Splash!" surrounds their hearing. The muddy water erupts near Kenny as a shadow forms on top of a rock that protrudes outward from the muddy water, and entangling debris.

Connie rubs her eyes; "I don't believe it! How? Oh my gosh! It's Murphy! It can't be!" She whispers to her self, "He died two weeks ago. Now I know, I am going crazy."

Kenny rushes over to the shadow as he reaches out with his hand to touch the shadowy object. He exclaims joyfully, "You're back...Oh boy! I've missed you!"

The shadow appears closer and shows his sturdy form. Murphy turns around towards the thick brush as he begins to growl, "Grrrr....Grrrr."

Kenny fluffs the dog's fur back and forth with amazement as he whispers to Murphy; "You're here! You're real!" He looks at his face and asks; "What's the matter boy? It's okay."

A bright, gold flash appears out from the water, and lunges at Connie and Veronica, knocking them under the water. The golden serpent coils it's rough, scaly body around both of their chests, churning them in and out of the water as it tries to squeeze the breath out of them. Murphy leaps into the water on top of the serpent, pawing frantically at the coiled beast.

Murphy's lip cringes exposing his elongating, sharp teeth. He latches onto the serpent's scales with his piercing bite as the twisting force from the serpent rolls Murphy into the water.

The water begins to rock from side to side as it begins to boil and spark. The serpent's death grip loosens as its scales steam into hot ash.

Connie, and Veronica fumble their way towards the thicker brush away from the electrifying serpent and climb out of the water coughing as they hold on to a rotting tree that has fallen across the swamp. Kenny rushes towards his sister lifting her up out of the water.

The fairies float, riding the rocking waves as they head towards a stationary log that is covered in vines. They pull themselves up and watch along the perimeters of the electrifying water.

The orange haired fairy squeaks, "Wow..That was a strong weapon you sent after the serpent! I knew you were warriors!...Uhh oh...I hope you have more powers, because Zulo is near, I can smell her!" The wind curls around the fairies wings, and the fog begins to clear. Black birds with three legs, and long sharp claws invade the trees, surrounding the swamp as if they were in a grid iron huddle formation mapping out their plays. Loud cricket sounds magnify behind the trees.

The evil witch, Zulo slithers around the brush to be seen. She allows her split tongue to clear a path down to the water. She speaks with a slow, crackling voice; "What do we have here? Intruders? I have not seen your kind in these parts, who sent you!"

Connie brushes the mud from her clothing, and speaks confidently; "We fell into the land accidentally, by reading one of your spells. So if you will be so kind, and help us back to where we came from, we will be so grateful...Oh and please release the King, and Queen, it's not polite to kidnap people...I mean fairies."

Zulo screeches in laughter as she bolts towards Connie; "Ha, ha, ha...pretty please, and sugar plums don't dance around in my head! You should not be so bold with your words to me, or I might just feed your tongue to my hungry little friends," she said, as her cold, crooked finger points towards the birds in the trees.

Veronica's eyes squint as she yells, "Don't you talk to my mommy that way! I'll feed you to my dog! You mean old bat!"

Zulo raises her hands motioning at her pet birds to circle in flight above them; "I'm tired of this meaningless chitter chatter." She creates lightning bolts to form a cage around Connie, Veronica, Kenny, and the fairies so that they can't escape. She opens her fist as a green glowing ball hovers over the palm of her hand. She closes her eyes, as she chants a spell. The wind churns hard, blowing the tips of the trees as far downward as they can go without breaking, thunder rumbles as it shakes the ground. Zulo's chants get louder with every word. She opens her eyes as they pierce yellow, and red towards the lightning cage. Her fingernails ignite with flames as she motions towards the fairies.

Just as Zulo gives the final command of her spell, Murphy jumps from behind her and knocks her to the ground, pinning her with his quick movements as he bites, and claws her back. Zulo falls to the ground on top of the flames that are igniting her from fingernails as they embed into her stomach. She squirms, clawing at the dirt trying to stand up. A fireball ruptures over her as she bursts into flames. The lightning bolts disappear around Zulo's unwanted guests.

Connie bends down, and places her arms around her children, holding on to them tightly as she cries, "We have our family back, even if we are stuck in this world!"

The Purple fairy tugs at Connie's shoe lace and squeaks; "But what about the King, and Queen? Will you still help us?"

Connie answers, "Yes, we will still help you."

Deep sounding horns rumble from a short distance beyond the twisted vines. "No need to continue the search, all is well!" commands Fairy King Alvery.

The King explains, "The witches' powers diminished, and so did her spell on us. Now the unicorns are safe, and our land is still protected thanks to you!"

Murphy leaps toward Kenny, and Veronica. He barks playfully as he wags his tail. He turns his face from side to side licking their face, not knowing which direction he wants to stay in.

Veronica kisses him on his head, and holds on to

his neck; "I wish we could all go home together boy. I missed you so much!"

Fairy Queen Martice climbs on top of Murphy's head, and looks up at Veronica, with an angelic voice she asks, "Home? Where is your home?"

Veronica responds, "California, next to the West beach. We don't know how to get back. We fell into a book that we were reading from this world."

"Maybe I can help, but my powers won't work unless you are warriors of our Kingdom, and will protect the law of the land of keeping the unicorns safe from harm." The Queen motions for the rest of the family to come closer, "Everyone, kneel before me, and look at me." She waves her tiny wand as she brushes it over their heads.

An array of sparkly colors beam around the family as if an oversized halo sits hovering above their head. The Queen commands, "You are brave warriors, who have saved our lives, and our Kingdom. The King, and I hereby make you soldiers of the fairies. You will be held in high honor for eternity, now rise, and accept my gift to send you home." She hands the wand to King Alvery.

The King waves the wand up, and down as he points to each person, then back towards the sky. The family close their eyes from the over powering sparkles and beams of bright colors from the wand. The purple beam expands on the ground as the blinding gold circles the trees. The swirling green, blue, and red beam glows straight up towards the sky forming a whirlwind, twisting and churning with high winds. Dark clouds form colliding into the mass. The whirlwind churns faster as it can no longer hold its stability. It explodes into the clouds, projecting colorful sparkles into the clouds and the sky.

Kenny opens his eyes and rubs his face. He focuses his attention in front of him and then he gazes around him. He picks up a pillow that rests on his bed, his mother rests in a chair next to the window in his room, and Veronica is sleeping under an oversized blanket on his bed. He looks around the room and with a sigh of relief he whispers to himself; "It was just a dream." He picks up the book that lays open on the edge of his bed and brings it closer to his face. Murphy's image is embedded on the page as he lay next to the King, and Queen fairy while they sit resting on their throne.

Kenny grins as he brushes his fingers lightly across the page, he whispers, "What a good boy."

<u>Writings in the sand</u>

When we were little, we played at the park, until it was
almost dark.
Writings in the sand, were our plans.
So innocent and pure.
How could we have known it wouldn't endure.

The world is a much bigger place, than the writing we had
placed
in the sand of paper at the park, just before dark.

But in our heart and soul is bigger you know,
that no one could erase.

I still wonder, if Melanie can remember after her death of
our embrace.
I hope one day it will be true.
Together, forever as we viewed.

Needing My Shadow

My life was complete
Filled with joy, love and peace.
We shared all that we had, and took care of one another.

So how could you leave me,
to dwell in this pain?
I hurt, I cry, I'm angered that you were stolen from me!

The pain you must have felt.
Shocking, sudden, flashing hurt.
I am sorry I was not there
To hold your hand, to stroke your hair
And to share this pain together.

Without you, Melanie
I am lost. I am empty.
I will not be complete.
For the days keep coming,
I wish I could go back
and take your place instead.

So Melanie, how am I to live without you,
when my pain runs so deep.
The loss of you not by my side, is too difficult to
understand or cope.

I don't want memories of yesterday.
I want memories of tomorrow!
I will never get a chance to joke,
or laugh in our special ways.
For you have another life to live.

But Melanie, I ask of you,
Look down from the Heavens and see all who loves you.
Your three sons, brother, sister, mom and dad, friends
and myself.

Please grab ahold of Reggie's hand and fulfill your new
lives together.
The way God sees.
For when my time on Earth is done, please Melanie, come
get me.

**Propelling Physics**

Caroline sat at her school desk straightening some papers as she placed them in her folder. The clock, hanging on the wall, ticked loudly, its noise echoed in her ears.

She gazed at the seconds as they disappeared into time. Mesmerized by the passing time she squints her eyes "I wish the clock would just stop working." she says to herself.

She twirls her brown, shoulder length hair with her small dainty fingers as her hands tremble, and her palms begin to sweat.

Caroline sighs as she looks around the classroom listening to the other students laughing and talking amongst themselves. Even though she is in the room, she feels like she is alone.

The bell rings loud as the students get up, chairs scraping on the floor. The grinding from the feet of the chairs sounds as if an orchestra were tuning up with high and low pitch horns blowing.

"Make sure you study tonight," the teacher, Mrs. West yells out, "we will have a test tomorrow!" The students filter out of the classroom in clusters, laughing and talking as they disperse to their next classes.

Caroline strolls slowly down the hall and walks outside the school. The students rush by her as they head toward the gymnasium.

"Come on! We have to get dressed and get on the field….it's kickball day!" Carolyn's friend Karen says as she waves to another student.

Caroline moans to herself, "Kickball..." she sighs sarcastically. "Yeah, I'll hurry on out there…oh what fun…"

The gym appears in Caroline's eyes as the building seem to grow ten times its size. The walkway begins to look as if it were floating in the air, as the foundation was moving up, and down. She reaches the doors to the gym, and pulls on the big, clunky, cold handles. A blast of cold air pummels her face as her ears fill with magnified noise from other students congregating inside. The fresh wax on the gym floor gleamed brightly, momentarily causing her to squint until she regained her vision.

Caroline made her way to the closed door with the sign decorated in pink, its bold letters marking the door as the 'GIRL'S LOCKER ROOM.' She looks at the door handle as she wipes her sweaty palms on her pants. She sighs "Okay," she whispers to herself, "here we go again." She opens the door, and immediately a musty stench filters in her nose. Shoes cover the floor; clothes bundled up in lockers.

"Uh oh!" Tina blurts out, "The superstar has arrived. You have two minutes to get changed, you dweeb!"

Some students laughed out loud and pointed at Caroline. Shiloh stepped in front of Caroline, her nose almost touching Caroline's face, "I don't know why you even show up for P.E.," she said,"You should go home, and get your mommy to write a note for you to sit out this class for the rest of the year. You're such a weak nobody!"

The students laughed, giving Shiloh a high five as they put their arms around each other's shoulders and walk out of the locker room.

Caroline felt her face grow warm as she looked down at her feet, trying to avoid making eye contact with anyone. She walked to her locker. She changed into her gym clothes. She neatly folded her shirt and jeans then put her clothes into her locker careful not to disturb the neat arrangement of her clothes. She placed her foot on the edge of the bench so that she could tie the shoelaces on her tennis shoe.

A whistle blows loudly from behind Caroline. She flinches at the high pitch sound.

"Move it Caroline! We don't have all day." the coach said impatiently. Caroline jogs out onto the open, grassy field where the other students are horse playing and laughing with each other The whistle blows again, "Okay. Shiloh, and Tracy... I want you up front and center! You two are the team captains...start picking your team mate's one by one." directed the coach.

Caroline, knowing that if everything went like it normally did she would be picked last looked down at her feet. She saw clogs of dirt popping out of bare patches in the grass. She hears names being called one after the other as the other students clap their hands, and cheer as they are picked.

Then there were only two girls left to pick for the teams to be complete, Caroline, and Karen.

Shiloh points her finger just beyond her chin and says, "Hmmm... ennie...meanie... minie... moe... Which one should I let go? Ha...I know, it's got to be you, Caroline who will be on..."

Caroline's eyes light up as her face glistens, "Yes," she whispers, "finally I get picked for something... anything."

Shiloh gazes at Caroline and smirks, "That will be on the loser wagon to go home...no way will I pick you. I'd rather have a player short than to pick you, ha, ha, ha, ha."

The coach blows her whistle, "All right...let's get into formation, and get this game started.

Tracy, you are the blue team, and Shiloh the red. Blue team take the outfield." (Why isn't the coach stepping in to stop the teasing? Or at least admonish Shiloh for her meanness?)
The coach blows the whistle, "Let's go...roll the ball."

The red ball rolls from the pitcher's circle as Tina kicks the ball low to the ground toward left field. The ball speeds past Caroline as she dives for it, then it spins away from her reach. Tina runs quickly to second base, and laughs at Caroline. "Dang! You are so slow! I'd hate to be on your team." Tina says, still laughing.

The next kicker on the red team kicks the ball up, which sends it toward first base. Tina trots behind Caroline, and makes faces behind her back as she makes it to third base.

She smirks at Caroline, "Hey....slow moe..." she says, "I'm going to score whether the ball is in play or not."

As she takes a long lead off her base she looks at Caroline, and winks. "This will be an easy score." Caroline rolls her eyes at Tina as she crouches down with a defensive stance.

The ball slowly spins toward the kicker. The kicker's foot connects hard with the ball as it spins in the air toward the infield of third base. Caroline runs forward, closing her eyes with her arms flared outward.

The ball is so high in the air it looks as if it has covered the sun. It loses its momentum as it falls downward in front of Caroline.

Caroline clamps down on her bottom lip with her top teeth as she turns her face to the side while the ball falls into her chest. She quickly opens her eyes, and glances at Tina where she slips on the base line towards home plate, trying to regain her balance to run back to third base. Tina seems to stop with her legs going in two different directions, and her arms wanting to touch the bases on the left, and right of her. She is frozen in place just for a moment as she looks to be in an old western stand-off. Caroline winds her arm back behind her body as she throws the ball at Tina with all of her strength.

"Ow! You did that on purpose!" Tina yells out as the ball hits her on the head.

"You're out!" The coach yells, "Take a seat Tina."

"But she hit me in the head!" Tina yells, "She cheated."

"Suck it up Tina that was a good tag. No rules this time on body shots, take a seat." The coach responds as she looks over at Caroline "Nice double play Caroline. Way to hustle!"

The coach claps her hands as she says to the students, "Okay girls, you can learn from Ms. Caroline's attention to the game...pay attention, and hustle. That's three outs, change sides. Blue team you're up at the plate."

The blue team was behind two points with a runner on third, and second. The winning run was at the plate. Caroline looked around, and noticed there was no one ahead of her in the line up to kick the ball. She wipes the hair from her sweaty forehead as she slowly walks up to home plate, kicking up the dirt with each step. She wipes the sweat from her palms on to her shorts. As she looks up the pitcher releases the ball. The bouncing of the ball begins slow, and then seems to speed up as it reaches home plate. Caroline kicks at the ball as it spins to the right of her foot. Caroline falls on her back and the dust lightly covers her body. She rolls onto her side not wanting to get up; knowing the other teammates will not let this one go. The coach runs over to Caroline holding her hand out.

"You're all right," she says, "let's try it again, this time keep your eye on the ball."

Caroline stands up holding on to her wrist as she tries to shake the pain away. The coach taps Caroline's back with encouragement, "Knock it out there girl, you can do it."

Caroline rocks back and forth anticipating the ball's release. She wipes the dust from her face with the back of her hand as she notices the chatter from the red team, they are not paying any attention to her. She readies herself to kick the ball. The players in the infield had their hands on their hips as the outfielders walked in closer toward the infield leaving the whole outfield open.

"Enough is enough." Caroline whispers encouragingly to herself, "Come on ball! Come on!" The ball rolls from the pitcher's circle again as Caroline's eyes beam onto the ball making its way to home plate. She takes a step forward; kicking the ball as hard as she can. The force of her leg connecting with the ball echoes across the field as it flies up in the air, and out toward the now empty centerfield. Caroline froze for a moment as she followed the path of the ball...cheers rang in the air as her team mates yelled for her to run.

Caroline ran down the base line to first base then, as she rounded first and headed to second she chanced a look to see where the ball had gone. Her eyes found the ball and realized that it had gone all the way past the outfield markers and was at the far end of the field. And then she realized that no one was anywhere near it! The girls from the other team were racing toward the ball, yelling at each other as they ran for it.

"A home run!" Caroline screams within her head. She keeps a serious look on her face as she trots by Tina and continues towards home plate to where her teammates are circled around the plate waiting for her to score the winning point.

Caroline jumps onto home plate, and is immediately covered up with pats on the head, and high fives meant for her.

Tracy puts her arm around her shoulder, "Nice comeback, Caroline!" she says."Say, me and some other girls are putting together a flag football team at the park after school. Do you want to be on our team?"

Caroline's eyes light up, "Yes," she immediately says. "I mean, sure. I'll check to see whether I have time. But I'm pretty sure I can squeeze in time at the park."

"Okay, we are meeting there at four," responds Tracy as she jogs with her friends back to the gym to change out of their gym clothes.

"Yes, I can't believe it,"Caroline whispers. Shiloh and Tina trot on both sides of Caroline as they block her in from entering the girl's locker room. Caroline's heart begins to pound harder in her chest as she stares at them, looking back and forth, not quite sure what they are up to.

Tina smiles at Caroline, "Say…you did okay in the game today. Maybe I underestimated you." Shiloh chuckles. "Yeah, me too, Maybe if you wouldn't drag in at the minute of the tardy bell in class, we can talk to you."

Caroline looks confused. "Well. .uh. .I guess I could get to class a little bit faster."

"So tomorrow for dodge ball, we want you to be on our team." Shiloh said.

Tina holds out her hand in front of Caroline, "I misjudged you."

Tina hesitated then said, "I'm sorry for saying mean stuff to you. Can we forget all that, and become friends?"

Caroline grinned happily and shook Tina's hand. "Sure," she said, "I guess so. We can see how things go."

Shiloh glanced at Tina, "Besides," she said, "we don't want to get our teeth knocked out by Caroline's death throw...ha, ha, ha."

Tina opens the girl's locker room, "Let's hurry up and get dressed so we can get out of this stinky locker room." She says. Caroline laughs as the door closes behind her.

Where Do I Go From Here

Spending the day like we always did,
planning ahead of things we dreamed.
Not knowing of what tomorrow will bring.
Until that day came crashing down, made my soul ring.

Where do I go from here.
I fall on my knees, praying to God that this is all a dream.
Where do I go from here.

Why did she leave?
Hearing words that float inside my head,
that your sister is now dead.
She didn't see the truck that was traveling fast and mean.
How could this be?
She was supposed to be with me!

Where do I go from here?
I fall on my knees, praying to God that this is all a dream.
Tell me, please tell me, how could this be?

We were always together, now we are apart.
Wonders of why run through my heart.

I'm still on my knees and I can't change a thing.
I can't let go.
Please God let me know of how this should all go.
Where do I go from here.

Now it's too late to show her my mistakes.
I thought she'd be here for us to grow old.
But now, I'm empty and cold.

You can't understand of what runs through my hands.

She needs to know that I am the weak one who needed her so.
Where do I go from here.

Twin-less

Am I dreaming?
Can this be true?
How can this happen on this morning dew?

Your life was shortened.
So sudden, so tragic.

Just as things changed for the better
Your marriage much sweeter.
Your finances stopped being a trap.
How can your life just end in a snap?

It's not fair!
It's not right!
How can your life end just before light?

How must we cope, with things we didn't do?
All the promises, plans were in the works for me and you.
I must be dreaming. It's a terrible one.
When can I awake to see your life still carry on?

Eye's of Red

Priscilla is excited to get home from a long day at school. Her mother is waiting for her to return from school so that she can help with their newborn puppies. Priscilla's long, curly hair hides inside of her red hooded jacket. She sits patiently towards the back of the school bus as other kids exit with each stop the driver makes. The sound of creaking doors pierce Priscilla's ears as if fingernails scrape across a chalkboard. She gazes out the window to view the playful squirrels chasing each other around in circles, and up the trees.

She sighs, "Gosh...why do I always have to be the last one to get off this bus, this sucks!"

The bouncing of the bus tosses Priscilla forward off of her seat as she grabs on to the top of the seat in front of her. She glances at the bus' rear view mirror, and comes across the bus driver's eyes beaming at her as if a lion has found its prey. She quickly looks away, hoping he had found a more interesting view to look at.

The bus driver asks, "Hey dear, are you okay?"

Priscilla's face warms as she looks up again and asks, "Are you talking to me?"

"Well, of course, everyone else has gone home to eat milk, and cookies. What do you have planned for this afternoon?"

"I'd rather not say. I just need to get home." replies Priscilla.

The bus driver grins as he chuckles, "I think I have an interesting idea for you to do?"

Priscilla's face sours as she rolls her eyes looking out the window.

"Don't you want to know what we can do?" asks the bus driver.

"Uh...no! I don't want to know...you're boring me, just stick with driving your stupid bus... stop looking at me you perve!" yells Priscilla.

Priscilla looks away from the driver as the cold glass from the window quickly sticks to the side of her face. She grabs onto the slippery glass with her dainty fingers as she regains her balance.

She yells, "What the hell! What is your problem?"

The bus driver smirks, "I'll teach you to show me some respect! All you little punks need some good old discipline."

"Hey! You creepo! Turn this bus back around! My house is the other way!" she responds.

"You, and I could have had something special, I see you back there giving me that innocent look. But you know there is something there." he says.

Priscilla stands up surfing the bumps as she makes her way to the front of the bus.

"I don't know what you're talking about! You sicko! Stop this bus. I have to get home, my mom needs me." she responds.

"Oh, I'll take you home alright." he says.

Priscilla's fingers embed on the rusting pole, as her body stiffens with fear. She glances at the houses racing by as they rush out of her view. Her breath becomes short, and heavy. Her eyes shift back, and forth, and all around on the ceiling, and back to the floor. She spots a fire extinguisher as if it was the pot of gold at the end of a rainbow. She grabs the cylinder frantically as she fumbles with the pin. She takes a deep breath, and pulls the pin out, while she pulls on the trigger. She sprays the thick, white foam in the bus driver's face.

The bus driver grabs his face, and eyes as he slams on the brakes, bringing the bus to a quick stop. The bus driver screams, "Ah! Why you little...."

Priscilla swings the fire extinguisher at his face as if she hit a home run with a baseball bat. The hard cylinder rumbles as it bounces off of his face.

Priscilla leans towards the driver's ear and says, "Like I said, stick with driving a bus you perve!"

She pulls on the slick handle, and opens the creaky door of the bus. She exits the bus, and runs in the direction of her house.

She runs down the sidewalk swinging her backpack over her shoulder as the pack absorbs the rough run and slips from her arm dropping on to the grass. She frantically looks behind her as she wipes her sweat from her forehead with the back of her hand. She stops, and bends over crouching over her knees as her breath is short, and fast.

A blue car appears in Priscilla's sight as the tires slowly, crunch the pebbles along the sidewalk.

A man's voice softly sounds from inside of the car and asks, "Is everything okay dear?"…"Do you need help?"

Priscilla's eyes open wide as she replies sternly, "Uh…no sir… I'm okay. I'm…I'm just tired from running, I'm almost home."

The man responds, "Well alright. Just wanted to see if you needed help."

"Thank you, but I'm okay." She replies as she continues to jog towards her house.

Priscilla's feet pound hard on the concrete while she runs up the steep hill that winds around towards her house. The top of the roof's pitch slowly emerges in her sight as the stained glass sparkles from the front of the loft's window. Her footsteps become quiet as she runs onto the thick, cool grass in her front yard.

Her mother, Cindy opens the front door to greet her daughter.

Cindy excitedly says, "Glad to see you, Cilla...these pups have been yapping for you for the last half hour." She looks at Priscilla's face and asks, "Why is your face red? What's wrong?"

Priscilla immediately slips into her mother's arms as she runs towards the front door.

Priscilla's voice muffles while her face implants onto her mother's shoulder she replies, "Mom...that freak bus driver!...He...he drove past my stop and wouldn't let me off the bus!"

Cindy presses on Priscilla's face gently with her warm, dainty hands. She looks into her crystal blue eyes as the sweat trickles down her forehead. She questions, "What do you mean, he wouldn't let you off the bus?"What happened?"

Priscilla pulls back from her mother's body as she continues to explain, "He said he wanted to teach me a lesson, and that I was always looking at him. Mom, I don't look at him! He's a perve! He wouldn't stop the bus, and was taking me in the other direction from our stop. I hit him in the face with the fire extinguisher, then ran off the bus!"

Cindy steps inside of the doorway and opens a

drawer from a small corner table as she grabs her Smith & Wesson 38 special pistol.

She sternly asks, "Where is he? Did he drive away?"

Priscilla points down the hill as she responds, "The bus was stopped down there. He was still on the bus when I ran away."

They run to the car, and drive down the hill as a cloud of dust spews out from the tires. Cindy drives quickly down the street. The streetlights appear green on the long stretch of the road. Priscilla fumbles at her seat belt, flicking the smooth material between her thumbs.

"There's the bus, what are you going to do?" asks Priscilla.

Cindy softly strokes the side of Priscilla's cheek as she grasps her gun she replies, "Oh..sweetie..I'm just going to have a little chat with Mr. Smith, and the bus driver. Now you stay here in the car."

Priscilla watches her mother walk gracefully towards the bus, and disappear out of sight as she enters the double doors of the bus. Priscilla's heartbeat thumps inside her ears. She blinks her eyes, and runs her fingers through her hair as she looks out of the car's rear window then back around towards the bus. She jumps as the car door opens. Her mother sits back into the driver's seat.

Priscilla's voice shakes as she gazes at her mother and asks, "Well...what did you do?"

Cindy drives slowly past the school bus and whispers, "He wasn't on the bus...did you see which way he may have went?"

"I don't know...he didn't follow me I don't think." Priscilla says, "Maybe he went down this way."

Priscilla looks out of her window as her forehead presses on the cool glass. She spots an over weight man with blood dripping from his face as he staggers towards the bushes that are along the sidewalk.

She yells, "There he is! Over there, near the bushes! Do you see him mom?"

Cindy drives her car onto the sidewalk. The car bolts up and down from driving over the curb. The car stops abruptly next to the bushes. Cindy jumps out of the car, and runs towards the staggering man.

She demands, "Hey! Stop! Are you the driver of that school bus?"

The bus driver looks around as he chuckles, "Are you talking to me?" He looks at the car glancing at the window at Priscilla who is staring in his direction. "You must have the wrong person."

Priscilla exits the car as she runs her fingers through her hair to push it out of her face. She walks slowly behind her mother.

Cindy demands again, "Why did you take my daughter some where else other than her bus stop?"

The bus driver explains, "She got home didn't she? So don't worry about it. Your daughter wanted to ride along with me..you know… kind of like extra credit..she is always talking sweet nothings to me, and giving me that look. You better keep an eye on that young lady..she's going to cause you trouble."

Priscilla clenches her fists as her voice screeches she says, "Mom he's lying! I don't even speak to that perve! He's a fat, slob! Let's just call the cops." Priscilla pulls her cell phone out from her pocket and dials 911.

The bus driver sniffs his nose as he puts his hands on his hips he motions to Priscilla, and says, "You kids are nothing but trouble! Look what you did to my face you little brat!"

Cindy draws her pistol, as she locks the hammer pin back and aims the shiny, silver barrel at the bus driver's chest she says, "I'm not waiting on the cops! You tried to hurt my daughter, now it's time for you to be handed your punishment!"

Priscilla waves her hands frantically at her mother as her voice shakes she says, "No mom! Don't do it. The cops are on their way…Just let his fat ass sit in prison where he can be a nasty perve all he wants!"

The bus driver smiles at Priscilla and comments, "See..I know you have me in your heart sweet thing." as he steps toward her.

Cindy swings her arm abruptly hitting the back of his head with the butt of the pistol. The bus driver groans as he falls to the ground lying still.

Sirens sound coming from behind them as a police

officer runs up to Priscilla, and her mother. He has his gun unstrapped from his holster. He immediately takes control of the scene.

The police officer looks at the victim on the ground, as blood is present on the concrete. He asks, "We got a call of a possible kidnapping? Is this the perpetrator on the ground?"

Priscilla replies, "Yes sir, he didn't let me off at my stop...and...he kept saying dumb stuff like..I..I always look at him and stuff. He wouldn't let me off the bus! I hit him with the fire extinguisher...I'm not going to jail am I?"

"No, you aren't going to jail. I need you to come to the station and fill out a report. But first, are you hurt? Do you need medical assistance?" asks the police officer.

Priscilla gasps and responds, "I'm fine. I just want to get away from that creep!"

Cindy walks to her car and puts her gun inside on the seat. She walks back to where the police officer is talking to Priscilla. She wipes the sweat from her face with the sleeve of her shirt.

She clears her throat and says, "You better be glad you showed up when you did. I was about ready to take the last breath out of him. But instead you can clean him up off the ground, and take this canine back to the pound where he belongs!"

"Ma'am, why don't you take your daughter home for a little while and let things calm down a little bit. Then just come to the station and fill out the reports we need okay? Besides, we have to do our investigation on the scene anyway. It will take some time." Said the police officer.

Priscilla grabs onto her mother's hand as she brings herself closer to her, she says, "Come on mom, let's go. Things will be okay now."

Cindy's eyes fill with tears as her voice shakes she asks, "Are you sure you don't need to go to the hospital?"

"No mom...I'm okay...Let's go home...remember the pups? We need to get back to them to make sure they are okay." says Priscilla.

Cindy puts her arm around Priscilla as she holds on to her. She lightly kisses her head. She says, "I'm so proud of you for getting away from that man...I would go crazy if I lost you."

Priscilla smiles and hugs her mom tightly she whispers, "Me too...I'd be crazy if I lost you too. Thanks mom for believing me, I love you."

Cindy helps Priscilla put on her seat belt in the car. She caresses her cheek as she smiles she says, "I love you too. Why don't we swing by the store before we go home? How about pizza and homemade milkshakes for dinner tonight? And maybe some s'mores for dessert? We can start the fire in the fire pit when it gets dark."

"Awesome! I can smell those roasted marshmallows now. But let's make your favorite milkshake..banana!...I want you to be happy too." Replies Priscilla.

Cindy sighs gratefully as she says, "You're such a sweet, thoughtful, and beautiful daughter. You're always thinking about making others happy. Don't ever change. Now let's get to that store!"

Three daddy's wrong.

I always had a dream of having a complete family.
But as we traveled down many streams,
it wasn't meant to be.

They never wanted to be around,
to see our little feet walking on the ground.

Tears filled my eyes,
hoping for the surprise.
That a daddy would finally show what a real man is to
know.

It was just three daddy's wrong.
Playing with our hearts.
Never stopped to see what he could have meant to me.
It was just three daddy's wrong.

As I look at my sisters and see how we are meant to be,
we still are a good family.
Stuck together through thick and thin,
I wish our dads were in the pen.

We can hold our heads up high to know that we will
survive.
We didn't need our daddy's fate of love he didn't embrace.
It was just three daddy's wrong.

A Writer's Hurdle

Words, rhymes, stories and lyric lines,
fills my head all throughout time.
Writing it down is not enough.
Having it perfected is the key.
Will it help only me?
Books and films are in the road ahead.
Making tough choices I do not dread.
I need to clear the way of all the quandaries,
from all those who uses us as prey.
My dream to write will not bend.
My soul still shivers to think it could end.
But my will is strong and my passion is long.
Will others view me as some one to seek?
And having projects that will be unique?
It takes one chance with only one glance,
to be a part with the strong at heart.
I am here, true as can be.
A lonely writer a waiting to see,
if she will be chosen to have the right key.
Could this be the right door?
Open my eyes and stand up tall.
Knock down the door with one big fall!
I am worth for all to see!
A writer will always live inside of me.